All the names of the characters in this novel are totally fictional and have no existence outside the imagination of the author. The characters in this novel have no relations whatsoever to anyone bearing the same name or names   The characters are not even distantly inspired by any individual known or unknown to the author. Although some of the incidents in this novel may sound real, they are totally fictional and completely invented by the author.   All the street names and locations are totally fictional and invented by the author and are totally not related to any real streets or locations.   Basically this novel is totally fictional.

THE INVASION OF THE DOOMS DAY CREATURES

BY

JAMES GORDON MASTERSON

Copyright number

TXu001247204

2005

All rights reserved. Under international copyright law, no part of this book may be reproduced, stored in a retrieval system or transmitted in any form, digital, electronic, mechanical, photocopy recording or any other form without prior written permission of the author or publisher.

This book was printed in the United States of America

Isbn: 9781973150527

Independently Published

CHAPTER ONE

THE BEGINNING

CHAPTER ONE

It was June 23rd and I was busy getting my camping gear out of my storage room and getting it loaded into my car. Tomorrow morning, I am leaving with a group of my friends, for a long awaited camping trip. We all just recently graduated from Procter Manson high School and we have been planning to take this trip for a long time, it almost seems like we have been waiting forever.

My name is Mike Ortman and I wouldn't miss this trip for anything. This might be our last chance to camp and party together before we all drift off and start our own lives as adults. My friends are Jerame Stone and his girl friend, Alice Topper, George Bateman and his girl friend, Mary Zigler, Mark Thompson and his girl friend, Betty Wilder and last but not least, my girl friend, Sharon Cordman. I have been working for hours trying to get all my camping gear into my car. I am already worn out and we haven't started our trip yet.

All of us are taking rifles and ammo, compasses, knapsacks and tents. We will be carrying food and drinks with us. All of the guys would be carrying the tents and most of the food in their knapsacks. The girls would be carrying the drinks. It was getting late so I turned in for a good night's sleep. Tomorrow morning, all of my friends will begin arriving and I need to get up early and finish loading all my stuff before they get here.

I had a good night's sleep, so now with day breaking outside, it's time for me to get up and get under way. I grabbed myself a quick breakfast, then I went outside to my car, to do a quick check and make sure all my gear was there. About an hour later, all my friends started arriving at my house. Thirty minutes after that, all my friends were here. All their cars were loaded with their gear and we were ready to leave.

We drove forty three miles until we came to an old street sign on Bratburg Road. The sign read "steep curve ". The sign was right on the outskirts of the Calandra forest. This would be our starting point. We pulled over all four of our cars and started unloading our camping gear.

After that, George, Mary, Mark and Betty drove our cars to a little store three miles down the road. We had made arrangements and paid the store owner in advance, to watch our cars for a week, while we were camping.

After they dropped off the cars, they had a three mile walk to get back to our starting point. The rest of us were just relaxing and watching all the camping gear until they get back.

We did manage to move all the camping gear into the forest and out of the sight of passing motorists, while we were waiting. About an hour and a half later, they did manage to arrive back at our starting point.

Everybody picked up their knapsacks and rifles and we got underway. We took compass readings while we walked and we were maintaining a direct southern course. Since none of us had ever been in this section of the forest before, this should be a fantastic adventure, a great learning experience for everybody.

Our overall goal was to make it at least ten miles deep into the forest, before we set up our first camp of the night. We knew going in, that we would never make more than ten miles the first day.

As we walked through the forest, we took notice of all the beautiful things, contained in this forest. A couple of miles deep into the forest, we came upon our first stream. The stream was roughly thirty feet wide and about two feet deep. It was too small to be a river and too large to be a creek. Standing beside it was six beautiful deer. We stood there and watched the deer for awhile until they spotted us and took off.

We took off our shoes and socks and made our way to the other side. After that we stopped for a short ten minute rest and then we moved on. Hopefully, with a little luck, we would make another three or four miles before it starts to get dark and we need to break off and set up camp. At roughly five o'clock in the evening, we stopped for dinner. We were all very tired by this time and we needed the rest.

We broke out some of the food and soda's that we were carrying and all of us sat down on the ground and had a relaxing meal. An hour later we were done eating and we got back on our way.

  We still have another two hours to walk before we set up camp for the night. As we walked, I kept thinking about my girl friend Sharon and how beautiful she looked. I had only started dating Sharon two weeks ago and we have never made love together. Tonight was going to be our special night.

  Finally eight o'clock in the evening had arrived and we spread out and started setting up our tents. The girls searched for small branches and twigs so we could get our camp fire started. After we set up the tents, the guys went out and brought in some big logs to throw on the fire. We got our fire going good and Alice broke out a bag of marshmallows. We sat around the fire eating marshmallows and telling jokes for about an hour, then one by one, we started heading for our tents.

Sharon was a very beautiful; five foot nine inches tall blond girl with big blue eyes. She came into my tent and lay down beside me. I started kissing her on her beautiful sexy lips. She had the most beautiful white tantalizing silky skin. Everything about this woman just drove me into a total love making frenzy. I found myself making love almost all night long, until four o'clock in the morning rolled around and I found myself totally exhausted. I rolled over and fell into a deep, deep sleep.

The next thing I know, its seven o'clock in the morning and time for all of us to get up, get dressed and get moving. I found myself being so tired and worn out, that I could barely get up at all. I managed to slide out of the tent and find myself a big rock to sit on. Moments later, here comes Sharon out of the tent, she's all pepped up, full of energy and raring to go.

I glanced over at the camp fire and noticed a pot of coffee brewing. I found enough energy, to make my way over there and get a cup.

Sharon is just full of energy, as soon as she exited the tent; she got busy taking the tent down and folding it up. She keeps looking over at me and laughing.

Early morning departure time finally rolls around and we are ready to get back on route and travel another ten or fifteen miles. Mark and Betty take the lead and we start traveling through the forest again. It didn't take long before I found myself pulling up the rear and trailing behind everyone else.

Sharon is up near the front of the pack and every once in a while, she will look back at me with a big grin on her face, laugh and yell for me to catch up. She's just having a field day picking on me now.

At one in the afternoon, we came upon a large swamp. It was as long and wide as the eye could see. We stopped and took a lunch break, while we decided what we were going to do next.

George and Jerame suggested that we stop here and set up our camp. It was quite evident that George and Jerame, just didn't want to get themselves muddy. Then Betty and Sharon spoke up and said; what are you, a bunch of sissies? Why should we let a little mud stop us? Let's just take our shoes, socks and pants off and walk right through the swamp. All the guys looked at each other and smiled and said; ok, that sounds like it will be a lot of fun. Mary and Alice wasn't too sure they wanted to go along with the idea, but after they saw everyone else taking their clothes off, they pulled their clothes off and the fun began.

We started walking into the mud and I found myself totally occupied looking at all the good looking girls, walking around in their underwear. Betty and Sharon took the lead and were guiding us across the swamp. I totally noticed that all the guys were watching, all the girls parade around in their underwear and all the girls were watching us too, doing the same. The mud was about four inches deep and very slippery. We were roughly sixty to seventy feet out in the swamp, when George slipped, spun around and fell flat on his face in the mud.

The rest of us started laughing so hard, that we could hardly stand up. George got really pissed off at us for laughing at him. When George stood up, he had mud from the top of his head, clean down to the bottom of his feet. We started calling him "the mud monster", and that pissed him off even worse.

The next thing I know, George picks up a gob of mud and throws it at Mark. It hits Mark right in the face and splatters all over the rest of us. Mark bends down and picks up a gob of mud and throws it at George and before I even have a chance to blink, I found myself caught up in the middle of a major mud fight. Everybody is now throwing mud at each other and there is no way to avoid getting hit, it's coming at us from all directions.

About ten minutes later our mud fight came to an end and we were all covered from head to toe with mud. Even our knapsacks and rifles were covered with mud. We continued through the swamp until we reached dry land on the other side. We climbed up a little two foot embankment and stepped out of the swamp onto dry land.

One by one, we came out of the swamp and we just plopped ourselves down on the ground and took a thirty minute rest break. All that walking through the mud and that awesome mud fight has totally zapped all our energy.

Betty and Mary were the first two to get up, and they started exploring. They strolled off by themselves for a short while and later they returned. Betty said; guess what we found. We found a river and it's only five hundred yards through those bushes.

We all jumped to our feet and made our way through the bushes, to the river. We dropped all our gear on the ground and all of us started to go in, when Betty yelled; let's go skinny dipping. I personally thought that was a great idea and so did everyone else.

Betty and Sharon were the first to remove their underwear and hop into the water. The rest of us watched them until they got into the water, then we took off our under clothes and joined them.

The river water was so clean before we got in, you could see clean to the bottom, all throughout the river. After we got in, you could not see anything, the river looked polluted especially after we washed all that mud off of us. We swam and splashed around for about an hour or more and we just had a grand old time. We even managed to get our dirty clothes washed, while we were in there.

Afterwards, we all crawled up on the bank and did some nude sunbathing, while we were drying off and waiting for our clothes to get dry. I guess we lay there a little too long because the sun was beginning to set, it would soon be dark and we haven't set up our camp yet.

We temporarily slipped our damp clothes back on and got busy setting up our camp for the night. We set our camp up roughly one hundred yards uphill from the river. It was starting to get totally dark and we had to scamper through the forest and find some dead branches, so we could start a camp fire.

We gathered up some larger logs and got our camp fire blazing. We all took a seat on the ground around the camp fire. We pulled some snack food and soda's out of our knapsacks and ate a little night time meal. Then Mark gets up and pulls his under shirt off and walks down to the river. He comes back a few minutes later with his under shirt soaking wet. He tears his under shirt into pieces and gives each of us a piece. Then Mark say's; clean all of the mud off of your rifles and out of the barrels before we go to bed. So, for the next hour, we set around the fire, telling ghost stories and cleaning up our rifles.

We couldn't help but notice how clear the sky was this night. You could see a million stars and it was extremely beautiful. Then we saw something weird hovering across the sky. We weren't sure what it was, but we thought it might be a small airplane. We could tell that it was in trouble and it was going to crash.

CHAPTER TWO

THE SEARCH BEGINS

CHAPTER TWO

 We watched the airplane come down and crash into the tops of the trees, about four to five miles away from our camp. Our first response was to call for help for the people on that airplane. So I asked; who brought a cell phone with them. Jerame and Mary both said that they had cell phones. Mary broke hers out first and tried to call for help, it wouldn't work, no reception. Then Jerame tried his phone, it wouldn't work either, again, no reception.

 The airplane crashed to far away, for us to try and find it, in the dark. So we decided to hunt for it in the morning. We took compass readings, to pin point the right direction to go in, at day break. Knowing that there was nothing else we could do tonight, we crawled into our tents and tried to get some sleep. Needless to say, I didn't get much sleep that night, because I kept wondering, if anyone survived the crash and they were lying out in the bushes, needing our help.

I finally dozed off around three in the morning, and I slept well for a couple of hours. The very next thing I hear is Mark yelling for us to get up. Sharon and I crawled out of our tent and went over to the camp fire. Mark already had a pot of coffee brewing and I poured me and Sharon a cup.

Everyone else was up and getting ready to start the search. We quickly finished our coffee and got ready to leave. We started walking through the forest, toward the designated compass readings, to search for the downed airplane. We were taking more compass readings every hundred yards or so, to make sure we were heading in the right direction.

We walked for many hours and still no sign of any downed airplane. We know that it has to be here somewhere, because we saw it go down. We decided to spread out into four groups and widen the search for the airplane. I told them to fire one shot if they find it. We spread out about fifty yards apart and resumed our search.

About thirty five minutes later, we heard a gunshot and we all headed towards the sound of the shot. We ran to George and Mary's group and we asked; what did you find? George replied nothing, we spotted a wild pig and Mary shot it. Then George pointed over to the bushes where the pig was lying.

I said; guess what George, since you two shot it, you get to stay here and build a small fire, skin it, clean it and cook it. The rest of us, are going back to the search for the airplane.

We spread out again and continued our search. We searched for another hour and a half with no luck, so we headed back towards the camp fire and the roast pig.

When we got there, George and Mary had the pig cut into chunks, skewed out on sticks and roasting over the fire. We were starving and that roast pig just smelled so fantastic. In a few minutes the meat was done and we ate like there was no tomorrow. I can honestly say that we really pigged out.

By the time the eight of us finished eating, there was nothing left but bones.

It was getting pretty late in the day and I didn't think that we could make it back to our camp, before dark.   So I suggested to everyone, that we camp right here tonight. This would leave us in a perfect position to resume our search tomorrow.

Everyone thought it over for a few minutes and then they all said ok. Sharon glances up at me and says; I hope it don't rain, and the rest of us replied; we hope it don't either. So we all took time to go out and gather some wood for the fire.

As sundown came and darkness began to set in, we had a huge fire going and we had plenty of extra logs sitting on the side. What we didn't have was drinking water, but that problem was soon solved, when it started pouring down the rain. Some nights you just can't win.

The rain was very, very cold and the fog set in very quickly. The fog was so thick, that you could not see an inch in front of your face. Thank goodness, that we had a huge fire going or we might have frozen to death during the night.

We spent the entire night huddled around the fire, just trying to stay warm. Needless to say, none of us got any sleep that night. The rain started to ease up around three in the morning.

After the rain stopped and the fog dissipated, just ever so lightly, a few of us got up and started walking around. A few minutes later Alice yells out; what is that? The rest of us came over to where Alice was standing and we could see it too. There was a light that kept blinking on and off. It appeared to be at least a mile, to a mile and a half away. No wonder we didn't find the airplane, we just didn't go far enough up the trail. We immediately took a compass reading, to get the correct heading.

Then we went back over to the fire and tried to get warm again. Around four o'clock in the morning, the ground around the fire had sufficiently dried enough for us to lie down and try to catch a little nap. We all lay down as close to the fire as we could possibly get. The next thing I know, I had dozed off into a deep, deep, sleep.

At eleven o'clock in the morning, Sharon starts shaking me and telling me to wake up. I opened my eyes and looked around and everybody else is already up and walking around. I slipped my shoes back on and rose to my feet. I was still very tired but it was time to get up and go.

Jerame called out; let's go find that airplane. Then George yelled; yeah, let's go do it. We checked our compasses and away we went. The bushes were still wet from the rain we had earlier. Right now, the sun was out and it was about ninety degree's. Still it's very uncomfortable getting our clothes wet again this morning.

We pushed relentlessly forward, through the bushes and underbrush. We were hoping that someone might have survived the airplane crash and that we could get there in time to make a rescue.

   As I walked through the bushes, I found myself wondering, what we were going to find when we got there. I kept getting this vision of finding bodies scattered all over the ground and human parts laying everywhere. To tell you the truth, I was actually afraid and feeling slightly sick, just thinking about what we were going to find.

   After a couple of hours of walking, we finally spotted the top of the aircraft and we slowly walked up on it. We stood there in a trance for a moment, and then we looked at each other. What is it? I mumbled, what in the world is it? We spread out and walked all the way around it. George spoke up and said; maybe it's one of our satellites that fell back to earth. Then Mark spoke up; it doesn't look like any satellite to me.

CHAPTER THREE

THE NIGHTMARE BEGINS

CHAPTER THREE

Then Betty spoke up; I think what we have here is a space ship from another planet. The rest of us looked in amazement for another moment or two. The ship was about thirty feet long and ten feet wide. It looked like three circular balls connected together. It had two long narrow fins, coming out of each side. It had a platform underneath it, but the platform had collapsed during the crash. There weren't any doors located on the top or the sides of the ship. Therefore, the door must be on the bottom of the ship.

Alice started banging on the ship and within a minute, she got an answer. We started hearing sounds coming from inside the ship. We looked at each other for a moment, then Jerame spoke up and said; holly cow, we get to make first contact, with an alien from another world.

We all got on one side of the ship and tried to turn it over. The ship was too heavy, it just wouldn't budge.

We changed positions and tried again, it just wouldn't budge. We started looking around for something to use as a lever. We spotted a couple of real tall thin trees. They were only about three inches thick. Now we have to figure a way to knock those trees down. George climbed to the top of one of those trees and he started throwing his weight, back and forth. With every thrust that George made, the tree came farther and farther over.

  Finally, the tree came close enough to the ground for the rest of us to grab it. Three or four of us grabbed it and brought the top of the tree all the way to the ground. The tree just popped and broke off.

  We carried the tree over to the ship and then we searched for a big boulder to use under our lever. With the lever in place, all of us pushed our weight down on it and tried to lift the ship. We were only able to raise the ship an inch or two. We needed another lever. This time Jerame climbed to the top of the tree and did his thing. About four minutes later, we popped that tree off, just like the first one.

We carried it over to the ship and grabbed another boulder and we were ready to go. We pushed down on the levers and the ship rose up to about twelve inches high. While the rest of us held the levers down, Mark went over to the ship, got down on his knees and searched for the door. He located the door, so he lay down on his back and slid partially under the ship.

He jerked on the door a couple of times, and the door opened up. The very next thing we heard was a blood curdling scream. Mark quickly jumped out from under the ship. He was holding his neck and screaming. We turned loose of the levers and went to help Mark. He had this thing, about the size of a small bird, attached on the side of his neck.

Mark got up and ran towards me, he was screaming and yelling for help. I gave that creature one really hard smack, but that little creature hung on for dear life. I smacked it a second time and the creature went tumbling to the ground. Mark was still screaming in pain.

The creature left a nasty bite mark and what appeared to be a long stinger. The stinger was about the size of a sixteen penny nail and the top of the stinger was wiggling back and forth.

   In a moment or two, Mark collapsed and fell to the ground. Everyone started yelling at me to pull the stinger out. I was actually afraid to pull it out, because it was lodged so deep in his neck. Everyone kept yelling to pull it out, so I reached down, grabbed a hold of it, and gave it one big yank. It slid right out and the wound didn't even bleed. Mark was unconscious by this time and had the look of death on his face.

   I picked up the dead creature and placed it and the stinger into a handkerchief and wrapped it up. I then placed it into my pant pocket. By this time, Betty was screaming and crying and holding on to Mark. I told Jerame and Mary to break out their cell phones and call for help. They both tried calling but their cell phones wouldn't work.

I told Jerame to take Alice and jog back toward Bratburg Road and to go as far as they needed too, to get that cell phone to work. I told them to tell the emergency personnel, that something bit Mark on his neck and he is in critical condition and you have no idea what bit him.

George remembered seeing a clearing about a quarter mile back and he thinks it's big enough to land a helicopter. The rest of us picked up Mark and we carried him back towards the clearing. It took all five of us an entire hour to get Mark to the clearing.

We laid Mark down, off to the side of the clearing. We checked his vitals and he was still alive, so we proceeded to build him a small fire to keep him warm and to help the helicopter pilot find our location. We gathered up a bunch of leaves and we were tossing them on the fire. Heavy smoke was coming off the fire and shooting up into the sky. This should help the helicopter pilot find our Location.

Betty went back over to check Marks vitals and she started crying and sobbing out loud. She yelled out; Marks dead, oh God, no. Betty lay down beside Marks body and placed her head on his chest. She just laid there and cried, and cried, and cried.

  The rest of us just stood there and looked on. At that very moment, none of us knew just what to say to poor Betty. I walked over and put my arms around her and tried to comfort her. Everyone else pretty much did the same thing.

  By this time, Jerame and Alice had jogged past the campsite and crossed back through the muddy swamp. Just on the other side of the swamp, they tried their cell phone and it worked. They placed their emergency call and reported what happened. They gave directions and requested a helicopter to transport Mark out. With help on the way, Jerame and Alice traversed the swamp one more time and headed directly back to their campsite.

Meanwhile, back at the clearing, everyone's sitting there, feeling really sad and waiting for the helicopter to arrive. Betty is still sitting beside Marks body and crying, when all of a sudden, she screamed and jumped up. She yelled out; oh my God, he moved, he's alive.

The rest of us jumped up and ran over there. Betty was right, his whole body was moving. We stood there and watched in total amazement, as his arms, legs and torso started twitching and jumping.

CHAPTER FOUR

THE BEGINNING OF THE END

CHAPTER FOUR

   Within minutes, Marks body began to burst open all over the place. Hundreds of those creatures began to emerge and they had wings and they were trying to fly. They looked just like the one that stung him. They appeared to be full grown and they were devouring his body from the inside out.

   They were making this God awful screeching, growling type noise. They had their wings flapping around as they devoured the rest of Marks body.

   All of us just panicked and took off running, just as fast as we could, heading back towards our camp. I kind of figured, as soon as those creatures finish eating Mark, they would be coming after us. Within a minute or two, I heard the helicopter flying over. We took off and ran for about a quarter mile, and then we stopped for quick rest break. We could see that the helicopter was going to land. I yelled out; don't land, please don't land. The helicopter landed anyway and the paramedic got out.

Within a second or two, the paramedic screamed and quickly jumped back into the helicopter. One of those creatures had latched on to the side of his face. About fifty of those things, started circling the helicopter and the pilot took off in a panic. With the paramedic laying unconscious on the floor of the helicopter and a large swarm of those things chasing the helicopter, the pilot done the worst thing that he could possibly do, he headed straight back to the Hospital. That large swarm of those creatures just followed the helicopter, straight back to the nearest city. The nearest city being Chandlesburg with a population of forty thousand or more.

Those creatures began diving down on the pedestrians and people sitting in their yards. They flew into open car windows. Nobody in the entire city was safe. When the initial attack was over, eighty three people had been bitten or stung. The ambulance personnel, being unaware of exactly, what was going to happen, carried the stung victims to three different hospitals. Two of the Hospitals were located in nearby cities. The paramedic on the helicopter was pronounced dead upon arrival at the Chandlesburg Memorial Hospital.

His body was taken down to the morgue for an autopsy. Fifteen minutes after his body arrived at the morgue, those creatures emerged from inside of him, and began flying, all over the basement of the Hospital.

There was seventeen employee's working in the basement of the Hospital and each and every one of them got stung.   The rest of those creatures flew up through a vent and escaped to the outside.

There were many creatures flying off in every direction. Within twenty four hours, there were reports from thirteen other cities, that strange creatures were attacking and biting people, all throughout the city limits.

The National Guard had been called in, and the battle to save all life on this planet, has started.   The National Guard had arrived in all thirteen of those cities and was using all weapons at their disposal, to try and stop the attacks from the flying creatures.

Meanwhile, getting back to us, we were running through the forest, heading back towards our camp, when Betty started calling those creatures, space hornets. The name sounded accurate and all of us started calling them, space hornets and the name stuck with us forever.

There was a large bunch of space hornets, circling over the entire forest. They were striking every living thing in sight. We passed a couple of dead dear that was recently bitten.

We slowed our pace down to a slow walk, and tried to remain hidden, beneath the trees. We slowly but surely, made our way back to camp. Jerame and Alice, were there waiting on us and they had no idea that the space hornets had become air born. They were sitting there right out in plain sight. It's a miracle that neither of them got stung. We linked back up with them and informed them about the space hornets. Then I told Jerame that we need to call home and find out what's happening out there.

Jerame told me, that his cell phone would work just fine, on the other side of the swamp. The big question is, how do we get there without getting spotted? As we stood there hiding under a tree, Jerame came up with a pretty good idea.

  His idea was to wrap a cell phone in a handkerchief and strap it to his back and then he would cover himself with mud from head to toe, and try to slide across the swamp. The rest of us looked at each other for a moment and then I said; that might work or that might get you killed. Are you sure you want to try it? Jerame answered; yes.

  We moved a little closer to the swamp, while staying hidden under the trees. However, the last twenty feet was completely out in the open. Jerame took his shoes off and waited for our signal. The rest of us peeked out and watched the sky and waited until it was empty of space hornets. We gave the signal and Jerame ran out and dove into the muddy swamp.

He rolled over and over, three or four times in the muddy swamp. He waited for our signal to return and then he got up and come running back.

Alice went behind a tree and removed her panties. She brought her panties over and handed them to me. I ripped the bottom out of them and had Jerame put them on overtop of his muddy pant. Then we slid them up, to his shoulders and placed a cell phone in them.

Jerame was now ready to attempt his little stunt. He was going to slide across the swamp on his stomach. Hoping to blend in with the mud and not to be noticed by the space hornets, Jerame slides out of the bushes and into the mud.

We watched as he got about thirty feet out in the swamp. All of a sudden, he rolls over on his back and looks up. Then he rolls back on his stomach and starts sliding again. So far he has been lucky, now he is about one hundred and fifty feet out and the space hornets haven't notice him yet.

We are keeping our fingers crossed for luck, as we watch him go. All of a sudden, we noticed that the sky was full of those space hornets and they were hovering, around and around, over the swamp. Then Jerame does the stupidest thing he could possibly do, he turned over and looked up again. The rest of us hovered beneath a tree and watched, as one of those space hornets flew down from the sky and bit Jerame right on the back of his neck.

We watched in horror, as Jerame screamed and yelled for help, but there was absolutely nothing that we could do. We stayed hidden beneath the tree until dark. As darkness arrived, everything got eerily quiet. All the loud screeching sounds had come to a halt and we could not see anything flying. Hopefully this was a good sign and the space hornets, sleep during the night.

We were desperate for food and water and we had to find some kind of safe shelter, so we ventured out from under the tree. We knew where the river was, but finding our way back to it in the dark, was another story. The forest was so dark that we could not see an inch in front of us, at any given time.

I was leading the group and I was trying to feel my way through the bushes, in the pitch dark. We were walking head first into tree limbs and stumbling over small bushes. Thirty five minutes later, we managed to find the river. The six of us, slipped down into the river and by putting our hands together and using them as a cup, we drank all the water we could hold.

After we got our fill of water, we talked for a few minutes and we decided to follow the river downstream. So we walked and swam our way down river. It wasn't as dark on the river as it would have been in the forest and we could almost see where we were going. We ran into quite a few logs lying in the river and we had to climb over or swim under, each and every one of them. After four hours of traveling down river, we stopped for a much needed rest break.

We climbed out of the water and we lay down on the river bank. All of us were quite worried, because we knew in three or four hours, when it becomes daybreak, we would all be sitting ducks, waiting to be picked off by the space hornets.

.

It was at this point, that a decision was made to leave the river and travel deep into the forest, and to search for a good hiding place, before morning. Again, we found ourselves feeling our way, through the trees and bushes.

During the night, we walked straight into a briar patch. As we tried to get out of the sticker bushes, we realized that they were blackberry bushes and they were covered with blackberries.

We wasted ten or twelve minutes, until each of us had picked a hand full of blackberries. We continued on with our journey, eating the berries as we walked. Every once in awhile, we found ourselves eating a bug, rather than a berry. It was hard to tell them apart in the dark. I bit into a real nasty, juicy bug and it just about made me sick.

As daybreak began to approach, we found a good hiding place, under a clump of evergreen trees. We crawled under the trees and went to sleep.

About six hours later, we began to wake up. One by one, we all got up except Mary. George went over and shook Mary, but she still didn't move. I ask George to check her vitals and he did. George yells out; oh my God, I think she's dead. Sharon checked her pulse and said; George is right, she is dead.

Our first thought, was one of those space hornets got her while she slept. We rolled her over and checked, and there was no bite marks on her anywhere. For some strange reason, she picked this time, to die of natural causes.

I couldn't help but think, that she was the lucky one, and by dying, she escaped from this endless nightmare, and left us here to carry on without her. Our hearts were filled with sadness and we shall miss her a lot. We said our goodbyes to her, and got ready to move on.

We slipped out from under the evergreen trees and checked the sky for the flying space hornets. The sky looked pretty clear, so we left Mary's body there and we moved on. We continued heading down stream and watching the sky as we walked.

   Following the river downstream, was taking us farther into the wilderness and away from all the nearby cities. It was kind of strange, but we weren't seeing any space hornets flying around.

   After walking for most of the morning, we decided to leave the river and head for a nearby mountain. We hadn't walked very far, when we spotted a young deer, standing under a tree. We only had two rifles left, because most of us ran off and left our rifles, when we saw Marks body bust open, and the space hornets emerge. I asked George to take the shot and kill the deer. In a few seconds, I heard a loud pop, and saw the deer fall. We ran over to the deer and we dragged it with us.

We dragged that deer for about three miles, until we arrived at the mountain. One of the first things that we spotted was an entrance to a cave. Alice suggested that we build a small fire and cook the deer, and we could check out the cave entrance later. All the rest of us thought that was a great idea, so we built a small fire, about one hundred feet from the cave entrance.

  We cut up the deer and started cooking it. About one hour later, we were feasting on the best tasting deer meat that we had ever eaten. All of a sudden, Sharon yells out; their coming, run. I looked up and saw a whole swarm of space hornets, coming our way. Betty yells out; run for the cave. We ran as fast as we could towards the cave.

  As we entered the cave, we encountered total darkness. We made our way about twenty five feet back into the cave and then we just sat down and prayed.

CHAPTER FIVE

THE RETURN OF THE DARK AGES

CHAPTER FIVE

Within seconds a swarm of space hornets flew into the cave. Just as we all thought we were going to die, a miracle happened. As soon as they entered the darkness of the cave, most of them turned around and flew back out. A few of them landed in the cave and become completely motionless. Our prayers had been answered, because none of us had been stung.

  After about five minutes of being totally frozen in our positions, we started counting the number of space hornets that had landed in the cave. We could see them because of the light coming in, through the mouth of the cave.

  We only counted three, so we decided to kill them before they get us. There were plenty of loose rocks everywhere, so we each picked up a good size rock and snuck up on the space hornets.

Bam, bam, bam, bam, bam, those were the sounds of those big rocks smashing the space hornets to death. Realizing that we could never leave the cave in broad daylight, we decided to do a little exploring and check out the cave.

It was pitch dark and none of us had any flashlights, so we started feeling our way through the cave. We asked for a volunteer to lead us through the cave, and George quickly volunteered. Each of us took hold of the person in front of us and away we went. I did the only noble thing that I could do and went dead last.

We were moving at a right nice pace of about ten feet per minute, when I got this awful thought, what if we get ourselves lost in here and can't find our way back out? Oh well, I just kept that thought to myself and just kept on walking. About thirty minutes, into the walk, I heard our fearless leader George, let out a yell, and then I heard a big splash. It appears that our three front people have fallen into a deep hole of water.

After I stopped laughing, I realized that this might be a good thing. I couldn't see, so I yelled out: George, who's in the water with you. George yelled back, I don't know. Then Sharon and Alice spoke up; it's us. Then I yelled out; is there any chance the water you fell in is drinkable? George replied back: I don't know but it sure is cold. Then Sharon replies; I think this water is running down through the cave, yes it is, it is running.

Of course, everybody knows that if the water is running, that's a good sign and it may very well be drinkable. We can't see what the water looks like, because it's too dark, and the way our luck is running, it will probably be running in from some swamp outside the cave.

I explained to everyone, that without drinking water, we are doomed and I asked for two volunteers to test the water. The next thing I know, they were volunteering me. They claimed that I hadn't done much lately and it was my turn.

I replied; no problem, who will join me? Sharon spoke up and said: I will join you sweetie. So I stepped down into the water and I waited for George and Alice to get out. Then Sharon and I, cupped our hands, dipped up some water and began drinking.

  Afterwards, we edged our way back to the cave entrance, where all of us laid down and rested until it got dark outside. Because we now know the space hornets get dormant after dark.

  As soon as darkness had arrived, we made our way outside the cave. George takes a rifle and tries to hunt some food, after awhile he disappears into the bushes. The rest of us, gather up twigs and branches, so we can build a fire.

  About an hour later, we hear two shots ring out and we know, George must have found us some food. A half hour later, here comes George and he is carrying a large opossum that he shot. While George skins his opossum, the rest of us light up a fire.

I poked a nice long stick through the opossum and we began to roast it over the campfire. After a few minutes, the smell of that roasting meat was just tantalizing. Meanwhile, we were all watching for the space hornets and hoping that they would not be attracted to our campfire.

An hour or so later, our opossum was fully cooked, and we took it off the fire and waited a few minutes, until it cooled down enough to eat. Then we began ripping pieces of the meat off, with our bare hands.

I couldn't believe how good that opossum tasted. It tasted a little like a pot roast, only it had hundreds of little bones in it.

We learned a very important lesson on this day, about the space hornets. We learned that when they roost for the night, they stay roosting and don't come back out until daylight. About this time everybody was dying of thirst, except for Sharon and me.

Under unanimous decision, we all decided to make our way back through the cave and drink our fill of water. This time I led the way through the pitch black darkness of the cave and I managed to stop right at the water hole without falling in. All of us lay down on our stomachs, cupped our hands and reached down into the water. We stayed there and drank water for ten straight minutes, until none of us could handle another drop.

Then we made our way back to the mouth of the cave. We found a nice comfortable spot and all of us fell asleep. The next morning, we all got up and peaked out of the cave. We saw a dead fox lying about fifty feet away and about ten minutes later we saw the fox burst open and around twenty space hornets emerged from inside. The space hornets began to fly around, looking for their next victims and they were hovering around the cave entrance

We have become totally confined to the dark inner structure of the cave during the day. Our only departure from the cave comes at night time, when we venture out and prowl for food. We hunt whatever animals are left to hunt.

But now we have a bigger problem, the space hornets that have emerged from the dead fox, fly through the forest during the day and their coming back here to roost during the night. There are about a dozen of them sleeping on a tree branch, right outside the caves entrance, every night.

This is our third night living in the cave and all of us are afraid to go out and build a campfire with the space hornets sleeping right over top of us. Our only choice was to venture farther out to a small clearing about eight hundred yards from the cave and take our chances building a campfire there. This became our regular routine and day after day, night after night, we did the same thing.

On our eleventh night we ventured out, George took a rifle and went hunting while the rest of us gathered wood for a campfire. We listened for gunshots most of the night and we never heard any. That night we went hungry because George never returned.

The next day, we spent a lot of time wondering what happened to George. I found myself wondering if George just couldn't take it anymore and he just took off and left us here and he made a break towards civilization or did he have a terrible accident and maybe he's out there lying in the forest somewhere and he's badly hurt.

On our twelfth night, we ventured out to hunt for food and look for George. This time all of us went on the hunt. We spent most of the night looking for George without any luck.

However, I did manage to shoot a couple of rats and we needed to hurry back, cook them and eat them before daylight.

After that night I found myself in sort of a strange situation. All the girls were lonely and they wanted to make love to me.

The strangest thing was that Sharon fully understood and she did not have any problems with me making love to everyone.

On our eighteenth morning of cave life, we made an important discovery. That morning we were all sitting around the cave entrance staring out, when we noticed one of the space hornets fall off the tree limb and hit the ground. Before the end of the day had passed, we witnessed everyone of those space hornets fall from the tree and hit the ground. That's when I knew for sure that the space hornets only have a fifteen day life span. They are born with one purpose in mind, " reproduce "and they only have fifteen days to do it.

Meanwhile, back in civilization and unknown by us, the creatures known as space hornets had spread to every country in the world. Mankind had tried every weapon in their arsenals, to no avail. The United States was the first to fall.

Ninety nine, point nine percent of all life forms on earth, which are the size of a rabbit or bigger, have been killed. The space hornets could reproduce a lot faster than mankind could kill them and that spelled doom for all mankind.

Within thirty days of the fall of the United States, all the other countries in the world began to fall. Then, strangely enough, fifteen days after the fall of mankind, the space hornets began to die.

The space hornets would pick up a straggler animal of some kind, here or there; just to continue their life forms for another fifteen days. Within ninety days of the fall of mankind, with no life forms left for them to eat, came the fall of the space hornets. As quickly as it started, it ended for everyone and everything except for us.

We are still living in the cave, five months or so have passed and we haven't seen a single sign of the space hornets in months.

CHAPTER SIX

THE RETURN HOME

CHAPTER SIX

All three of the girls are pregnant and we are considering trying to walk out of the forest and head back to civilization.

So one cold day in November, we left our cave for the last time and began our long walk back home. We ventured into the forest and just kept walking. Hours later we came upon the river and we began to follow it back towards home.

A short time later, we came upon a deep hole of water, alongside the river. The hole was totally isolated from the river so there was lots of fish trapped in the hole. We decided to stop here and catch ourselves a meal.

The four of us took our shoes off and waded into the water. We started grabbing the fish and tossing then up on the bank. Before long we had tossed eleven fish out of the water. We cleaned the fish and then we built a campfire.

We rammed a stick through each fish and roasted them over the open fire. In a short while, they were done and we started eating them. These were the first fish that we've had within the last six months or so, and boy did they taste good.

  After dinner we continued on our way. We walked for a couple more hours and it started getting dark. We found a nice comfortable place to lie down in a patch of high weeds. All of us soon fell fast asleep, and we were sleeping like babies until along about midnight, that's when I woke up and I was freezing.

  It had really gotten cold out here and I was just sitting up and shivering. Soon the girls began waking up and they were shaking and shivering too. We huddled as close together as we possibly could in an attempt to use our body heat to get warm. It seemed like this night would never end as we lay there freezing our tails off all night. Morning finally arrived and I could only think of one thing, that I never, ever, want to go through another night like that one.

The morning wasn't much better; it was still as cold as hell out here. We were up and walking around, but we were still half frozen. As we walked and walked, the temperature kept getting colder and colder and we were totally miserable. I knew that if we didn't find some shelter soon, some of us were going to freeze to death.

After a couple hours of walking, we once again encountered that space ship that had those horrible creatures in it. My first thought was that we could turn over this little ship and use it for a shelter, so I spoke out and said; let's try to roll the ship over onto its side and get the doorway facing up so we can use this ship for a shelter.

Everyone agreed, so we began our attempt to roll the ship over. The two trees that we used as levers before were still there, so three of us applied a little weight, while the fourth shoved rocks under the ship. We were slowly raising and tilting the ship, up and over.

For the next four hours, we kept shoving more and more rocks under the ship until we finally got it to turn over on its side. We opened up the door and went inside. The first thing that we noticed was the partial remains of two dead aliens and a bunch of dead space hornets on the floor. The very next thing that we noticed was that the inside of the ship was about thirty degrees warmer than it was outside.

  There were two strange red meters located in the front of the ship and a very large book written in some unknown language, sitting in a small rack on the side of the ship. I think this book must be the ships log.

  Anyway, we made ourselves comfortable, rested up for a couple hours and got warm. Then we got to wondering, if the two rifles and the ammo that we had to leave in the clearing, when we were forced to run five months ago, would still be there. The clearing was about one mile away so we decided to go look. Halfway to the clearing, it started snowing pretty heavy.

We continued walking until we arrived at the clearing. By that time there were four to five inches of snow on the ground. Since everything was covered with snow, the girls and I spread out and started dragging our feet across the clearing. Within a few minutes, we had uncovered two rifles and one knapsack. The rifles were both rusty and dirty and the knapsack was frozen solid.

We took our newly found merchandise and headed back toward the ship. The snow was coming down heavier and heavier. By the time we spotted the ship there must have been fifteen to sixteen inches of snow on the ground.

After we re-entered the ship and got warmed up a little, we started cleaning up the rifles. The knapsack was full of wet, rotting clothing and two boxes of ammo. I wasn't too sure that the ammo would be any good after being out in the elements for five months. Later that night, I took one of the rifles and loaded it with our newly found ammo and went out into the snow to hunt for food.

I was only out about five minutes when I spotted a rabbit. I took aim on him and pulled the trigger. The first bullet was a dud, it wouldn't even fire, and so I ejected it and tried again. The second bullet fired, made a little ping, went about thirty feet and hit the ground.

I was totally disgusted after that, so I went back to the ship and got some good ammo. An hour later I came back out and returned to the hunt. This time I spotted a large opossum and I took aim and shot him. I have really grown to like the taste of opossum over the last five months and I couldn't wait to get back and cook him.

After I arrived back at the ship, I realized that we would never be able to find any firewood in the snow, so I skinned him and cleaned him and buried him deep in the snow, right next to the ship. The next morning, we all went out to hunt for firewood. This was not an easy task because all the twigs and branches were buried deep in the snow. But somehow we managed to find a good supply of wood, and we carried it back to the ship.

We cleared a spot in the snow and piled twigs and branches on it. Ten minutes later we had a pretty good fire going and I dug up the opossum from the snow and began to cook him.

   We were all standing around the fire when Alice looked up and said; what's that? The rest of us looked up and saw a flock of something flying straight toward us. In a blind panic, we all ran back into the ship and slammed the door. Later we realized it was just a flock of sparrows and not those nasty space hornets that we were so worried about.

   By the time we returned back outside to the fire, our opossum was burnt to a crisp on the underside. The top half of the opossum was still in good shape, so we cut it into four equal pieces and we ate it for breakfast. Later, we returned to the ship to relax awhile and I decided to unbolt those two red meters from the wall. I have no idea what they are, but I am going to take them and the book with me, when we leave.

We stayed in the ship for three more days until the weather broke and it warmed up a little. Then I packed up those two red meters and that book and we started our walk back towards civilization.

I kept wondering what we would find when we got there. Would any of our family members still be alive? After walking for seven straight hours, we stopped to hunt dinner and make camp for the night. We had arrived back at the edge of the swamp and none of us wanted to get covered with mud before going to bed.

We built a nice fire and went to bed. It got pretty cold that night but the fire kept us warm. Every two or three hours, I would get up and throw some wood on the fire to keep it going. The next morning finally arrived and we got up for an early start. The muddy swamp was slightly frozen over so when we crossed it, we didn't even get muddy. We started walking hard and fast knowing this was our last day of walking and we will exit this forest sometime today.

Four or five hours soon passed and I knew that we should be coming up on Bratburg Road any time now. Finally we walked over a small embankment and there it was. We stepped out onto the street and stood there a few minutes and looked both ways. There wasn't one single car coming from either direction, so we started walking down the road towards the little store where we left our cars parked.

CHAPTER SEVEN

THE FACE OF REALITY

CHAPTER SEVEN

We walked for twenty minutes or so, when we spotted a car about three hundred yards ahead, off the road and in a ditch. The girls and I kept walking until we arrived at the driver's door of the vehicle. Inside the car were the skeletal remains of the driver. This was truly a bad sign because if there were any people around, they would have removed the body.

We continued walking until we arrived at the little store. All the doors were open but there wasn't anyone in the store. I yelled out a couple of times but no one answered. Fortunately for us, all our cars were still there, however, we only had one set of keys and that was the keys to my car. The battery in my car was completely dead so we went back into the store and waited awhile to see if the clerk or the owner shows up. Then we started looking around and noticed that most of the food in the store had gone bad. At this point we knew that the owner wasn't coming back to the store.

All the lunch meat was covered with mold.   Their refrigerated compartments weren't working.   Pretty much everything in the store was either bad or totally stale.   We helped ourselves to some stale candy bars and some hot soda.

   Since there wasn't any way to charge my car battery or obtain a new one, we started walking again.   We had only about forty more miles to go, to get back to our home town.   After walking another two or three miles, we decided to make camp for the night.   We were still near the forest so we walked about twenty five feet back into the trees and set up camp for the night.

   The girls gathered some twigs and branches, while I gathered some heavy logs.   Betty got the fire going while the rest of us moved all the small rocks and pebbles out of the camping site.   We talked awhile before going to sleep and we discussed the fact that not a single car has come up or down the road all day.

The next morning we all got up early and started walking to the next town. I figured that we were only about one mile away from the next heavy populated area. Thirty five minutes later we entered the outskirts of that small town.

We could see skeletal remains all over the place. The entire town was so eerily quiet. There was no sign of life anywhere. We continued walking for another quarter mile until we arrived in front of a large hardware store.

I broke one of the windows out of the store and we went in. Sharon grabbed a cart and we got us a generator and a battery charger, then we pushed our cart out into the parking lot. Right next door to this store was a sporting goods store, so we walked over there and broke a window out. We went inside and got us some new rifles and ammo and night vision goggles. We left that store and went back out in the parking lot. We walked around the parking lot looking for a vehicle with keys still in it.

Alice located a sport utility vehicle that had the keys in it. Of course the skeletal remains of the driver and a passenger were still in it. Sharon and Betty removed their bones while Alice and I went across the street to the gas station and got some gas for our new equipment.

We came back to the vehicle and cranked up the generator, plugged in the battery charger and started charging the battery. Twenty minutes later the battery was fully charged so we loaded up all our gear and drove back across the street to the gas station. We filled the tank up and off we drove.

As we drove down the highway, we could see bones everywhere. About a mile farther down the street, there were six or seven cars abandoned in the middle of the road. I had to drive around two houses, and I drove right through their yards to get around the blockade. We continued on down the highway and there was no sign of life anywhere. It was kind of like driving through an endless cemetery.

There was a strong smell of death in the air and it was so bad that it almost made me puke. We drove on down the highway avoiding abandoned cars left and right. A short time later we arrived at Alice's house.

Every one of us got out of the vehicle to go inside. As we walked up into the yard, we could see broken windows all over the house. Alice opened the door and we all went in. On the couch was the skeletal remains of a woman and then we walked into the kitchen and found the skeletal remains of two children.

Alice's entire family was here and they were all dead. I put my arms around Alice and tried to comfort her and she just burst in to tears. Sharon and Betty came over and tried to comfort her but she just kept on crying.

Deep in my gut, I knew all of us would find the same thing when we got to our houses. We all got back in our vehicle and headed to Sharon's house.

Ten minutes later we arrived at Sharon's house and her house was empty. I guess her family must have made a run for safety. Next we drove to Betty's house and she found the remains of her entire family inside. With all the girls crying, we made our way to my house and there I found my entire family dead. I was unable to hold back the tears any longer and I found myself holding onto the girls and crying like a baby.

After an hour or two, we all calmed down and tried calling people on the telephone, who lived in other states. All the phone lines appeared to be working. We kept hearing the telephones ringing but no one answered any of our calls.

Sharon turned the television on and all the stations were blank. They were being broadcasted, but there was no picture on any station. I have a satellite dish here at my house and for this to be happening, it leads me to believe those creatures wiped out the entire population of the United States and who knows how many more countries.

All of a sudden we realized that the four of us may be responsible for wiping out the entire population of the world. Billions of people may be dead because of us. We looked at each other and all four of us started feeling sick to our stomachs. If we had only left that space ship alone, at least for another fifteen days until all those creatures had died.

Then we started thinking that there must be other survivors out there somewhere and all we have to do is go out there and find them. We decided to get a good night's sleep and in the morning we would venture out on a search mission and try to locate some other survivors.

The next morning, we got up and opened up a couple cans of different meat products and ate them for breakfast. Betty also made a pot of coffee and we drank every drop of it before we left. We armed ourselves with fully loaded rifles, just in case of the event that we do find some survivors and they are hostile. Sharon suggested that we do a house to house search.

We ventured on down the street checking every house as we go. We spent the entire day searching houses and we did not find any people that were still alive. It's now getting late so we are going to call it a night and return to my house for dinner.

   Tomorrow, I think we are going to check the sewers and see if anyone is hiding down there. After all, the sewers would have made the perfect hiding place.

   Betty opened up some can food and we had dinner. Then we had a little meeting and discussed upcoming events. The stench of death is just too much to bear in this house and in this neighborhood, so tomorrow morning just before we start our sewer search, we are going to find us a new house to live in.

   Since all three of the girls are pregnant and there aren't any doctors to deliver the babies, we discussed going to the library and getting some books on how to deliver a baby.

After the meeting, we were pretty tired so we all turned in early and went to bed. That night we all slept like babies and got a good night's rest. Bright and early the next morning, we all got up and ate breakfast. Then we loaded up all our gear into our vehicle and we left to go house hunting.

We drove about four to five miles to a wooded area outside of town, where we found a beautiful mansion, located back in the woods and no other houses anywhere near it. I pulled into the driveway and we went inside to check out the house. It was beautiful, it had six bedrooms, three bathrooms and nothing but woods all the way around it. But the most important thing of all was, the air was fresh, there were no bodies in the house and no stench of death in the house.

Sharon started unloading our gear and bringing it inside. The rest of us went outside and gave her a helping hand. After we got all our gear inside, we stepped out into the back yard and we saw four rabbits out there playing.

Our newly acquired woods was chucked full of rabbits. I ran inside and grabbed my rifle, came back outside and shot a couple of those rabbits. We are going to have fresh meat for lunch.

I sat outside in the back yard and cleaned and skinned those rabbits, and then I passed them off to the girls for cooking. Later the girls called me to come inside for lunch. The girls had prepared rabbit stew and boy did it smell good. We spent about an hour relaxing and enjoying our lunch and just talking to each other.

Afterwards, I walked back through the house and noticed that all three girls had put their stuff into one bedroom. I called the girls together and explained to them, that the idea of having a lot of bedrooms was so each of us could have our own bedroom. The girls were not happy about getting their own bedrooms, but each one of them took their belongings and moved into another room anyway.

After all the confusion, it was finally time to go check out the sewers for any signs of life. We drove back into town and stopped next to a sewer entrance. I got a tire iron out of the back of our vehicle and popped the sewer lid off.

I told the girls to stay topside while I go down and check out the sewers. Down the sewer I went, I took a quick look around and then I headed off down the pipe. It wasn't long before I came across a couple bodies and they did not look like they were killed by the space hornets. By the looks of them I figure they either starved to death or drowned.

A little further down the pipe, I encountered a large intersection and the pipe branched off into five different directions. I took a good look around and the pipe I just came through was larger than these five pipes, I chose to take the center pipe and I continued on.

After many hours of searching, I came to the conclusion that there weren't any living people down here, just corpses. I turned around and headed back towards my exit spot where the girls were patiently waiting. It took me close to three hours to get back to that spot. When I climbed up the ladder to exit, it was already dark and the girls were nowhere to be found.

CHAPTER EIGHT

MY WORST NIGHTMARE BEGINS

CHAPTER EIGHT

   Shortly after I exited the sewer it started pouring down the rain. I noticed the automobile was gone and I figured the girls gave up waiting for me and went home. After yelling for the girls four or five times, I was sure that all of them had left and I went walking down the street in search of shelter.

   Two blocks down the road, I found an unlocked car and I got into it. By this time I was soaking wet and it was getting colder by the minute. It wasn't long until the rain turned to snow and I was freezing. About ten minutes later I decided to enter a house and get warm. I entered the house and found everything that I needed to get warm. I found coats, blankets and lots of sweaters in the house and that's where I spent the night. I did not get any sleep because I was too worried about the girls. The next morning, I got up early and started walking back to our new house.

It was a five mile walk and it was freezing cold outside. There was six inches of snow on the ground and the wind was blowing about thirty miles per hour. Nothing seemed to bother me because I had only one thing on my mind, were the girls okay? Two hours later I made it to the front door of our new home and our automobile wasn't there.

I went inside and looked around to see if they had been there and left. Their beds hadn't been slept in and it appears as if they never came home. Now I am really worried. I hung around the house for the next couple of hours and just watched out the window for them.

When I was sure that they weren't coming back to this house, I put on a coat and started walking back towards the sewers. I was seriously hoping and praying that when I get there, that I could figure out what happened to all of them. I could not imagine living in a world all by myself. By this time the temperature had dipped and it was so cold that I thought I was going to freeze to death. I was trembling and shaking from the cold as I walked.

I was walking as fast as I could possibly walk with my hands in my pockets and my head dipped low to keep the wind out of my face. An hour and a half later I arrived back at the sewer and there wasn't a sign of them anywhere. It wasn't until I looked down and noticed tire tracks in the snow that I realized that they came back here after I had left. The tire tracks headed back into town and so I started following them. Two miles later, I spotted our vehicle parked in front of a house.

I walked around the rear of the house and peaked into the window to make sure they were alone. There was always the possibility that there was another survivor and he had taking them prisoner.

It didn't take me long to realize that they were all alone in the house and crying their heads off. I walked back around to the front door and knocked. Not a single sound came from the house for the next couple of minutes. All of a sudden the girls came from the rear of the house with their rifles in their hands. They scared the living hell out of me.

The moment they realized who I was, they dropped their rifles to the ground and ran over and started hugging me and kissing me. The girls were crying and in a moment I found myself crying too. We all went inside the house and I asked them, what happened?

The girls told me that they were hungry and they left to get something to eat. They returned right away and they waited for hours for me to come out of the sewer. Then when it started raining real heavy and the sewer began filling up with water, they thought that maybe I had drowned. They could not find their way back to our new house because none of them watched where we were going, when I drove them over there. I told them my story and we all had a good cry.

We spent the night at that house and mostly talked and cried all night. The next morning we drove to a grocery store and picked up a large supply of can food. Then we returned back to our new home.

Later Sharon and I drove to a computer store and I picked up a top of the line computer. We did not have any electricity so I had to crank up the generator each time I used my computer.

I began to study the log book from the space ship and those two red meters. The space men had a language like no other on this earth and I was determined to decipher it.

We settled into our new house and the years began to pass slowly. Our family had grown pretty large for a total of four adults and seventeen children. In all this time we never discovered another survivor anywhere.

Then one day I made the discovery of a lifetime, I managed to decipher the language of the spacemen. Using my computer, I began translating and rewriting the entire book into English.

CHAPTER NINE

DISCOVERING THE TRUTH

CHAPTER NINE

   While deciphering the ships log into English, I discovered that those creatures were a dooms day device genetically created by another world and launched against their world. With no hope of surviving the attack, they launched a time ship to go back in time one year and warn the people of the upcoming attack.

   The two spacemen launched their ship back in time unaware that one of those creatures had somehow gotten aboard. After the first spaceman had gotten bit, the second spaceman had no choice but to turn his ship away from his planet. Within a few hours the second spaceman had gotten bit.

   The ship was traveling at a speed of five million miles per hour and somehow crashed on our planet. I also discovered that the two red meters were the time machines that allowed them to go back through time and that time travel causes the hull of the ship to heat up to three hundred degrees.

Finally, at my disposal I had the technology to go back in time and set the world straight. The four of us, Sharon, Betty, Alice and me were all personally responsible for killing the entire population of earth. All because we opened the door on that space ship and let the creature out.

I called a meeting between the four of us and we discussed what we could do and what we should do to set things right. We all loved our children very much and if we go back and prevent those creatures from getting out of the ship, then nothing from this world would exist anymore and all our children would vanish.

However, if we don't go back, our children of this world would be lonely and never have anyone to love and marry. All they would have is each other and all our future generations would probably be derived from incest. All of us have a guilty conscious about what we have done and we could set the record straight. We took a vote on what to do and we had a tie. Betty and Alice voted not to go back and Sharon and I voted to go back and make the change.

    However for now, we decided that we would not do anything and we all went back to living out our everyday life, in this time and in this place.

    Both Betty and Alice were both worried that Sharon and I would make an attempt to go back in time.   They were getting very paranoid and I was afraid that they would destroy my two red time travel machines.   I eventually took the two time machines out and hid them in a house about a mile down the road.   The girls would soon get tired of looking for them and give up the search.

    Meanwhile, Sharon and I were making plans of our own.   We drove sixty miles to a space research lab and commandeered two space suits capable of withstanding temperatures of up to five hundred degree's.   Then we drove to an auto parts store and picked up a couple of new car batteries and a container of sulfuric acid so we could charge them up later.   Then we drove to a hardware store and picked up another generator and battery charger.   Our last stop was at a surplus store for a couple new knapsacks.
.

CHAPTER TEN

CHANGING HISTORY

CHAPTER TEN

Sharon and I took our newly acquired merchandise back to the house where I had hidden the two time machines. We charged up the batteries and tried on the space suits. After that we went home and just tried to act casual around the other two girls.

The next morning we went to a gun store and got us a couple of guns and a hundred rounds of ammo each. We also got two GPS hand held tracking devices and a large camouflage quilt. Then we went to a motorcycle shop and got two all terrain vehicles and two trailers that we could pull behind them.

After we had everything that we would need, we went back to our house and ate dinner with the other two girls and our children. Betty and Alice got us alone and made a last ditch attempt to talk us out of going.

The next morning Sharon and I got up pretty early and walked to the house where our gear was stored. We loaded everything into the trailers and drove off. When we got to the steep curve sign on Bratburg Road, we turned off and entered the forest.

Everything was going pretty good, we found the swamp and drove right through it. We continued on our way through the forest. Sharon and I drove for many hours and we could not locate the spaceship.

The two of us was getting pretty hungry so we stopped and took a break. I saw a rabbit and I shot it with my pistol. Sharon built a campfire and we cooked the rabbit and ate it. We drove and searched for another three hours with no luck at all. It was starting to get dark so we needed to find a good camping spot for the night. Sharon found a nice smooth grassy spot and we decided to spend the night there. The next morning we realized that we had forgotten the two most important items and we had to go back to town and get them.

We spent the next five hours making our way back to Bratburg Road. Then we drove back into town, stopped at a store and picked up a couple tents. Afterwards, we went house to house collecting money. By the end of the day we had collected about twenty thousand dollars. We would definitely need that when we got back to civilization. Sharon and I split the money up fairly and called it a night. We stayed in town at one of the houses and got a good night's sleep.

The next morning we ventured back into the forest. After passing through the swamp, we headed deeper into the forest. Three hours later we managed to locate the spaceship. I informed Sharon that the ships log said that these time machines weren't very accurate and they could be as far off as ninety days.

Using our belts, we strapped the time machines around our waist and we loaded the batteries into a pouch on the knapsack. Then I set the dials on the time machines for an eleven year six month decent. I allowed three extra months to make sure we did not materialize right in the middle of those creatures and get ourselves killed.

We placed all the rest of our gear into the knapsacks and placed the knapsacks on our backs. Then we hooked each other's wires from the batteries to the time machines. I hooked hers and she hooked mine.

I pointed at the big tree in front of the ship and instructed Sharon to hang a piece of clothes on the limb, with the date you arrive, immediately after you get there, and I will do the same. Then I told her that all she needed to do to get the date, was to turn on the " GPS ".

Sharon gave me a big hug and kiss and then we put the space suits on. Standing face to face, I began the count down from three. As soon as I called the number one, both of us hit the button.

Away we went soaring through time. All I could see was black and white flashes of night and day. I began getting extremely dizzy and fell to the ground. Then I upchucked two or three times inside of my spacesuit and felt like I was going to die. The journey took around fifteen minutes and I thought it would never end.

After lying on the ground for another five minutes, I finally got up and took my spacesuit off and got my " GPS " out. Sharon wasn't here yet so I took a piece of clothing and wrote the date on it and hung it on the limb. I had arrived here four months before the spaceship would arrive.

I unloaded my tent and set it up about one hundred feet from where the spaceship would crash and I patiently awaited Sharon's arrival. Day after day, I hung around camp and watched for Sharon. I only left camp long enough to hunt food and water.

After six days of waiting, I could not wait no more. I took a " GPS " reading on where the spaceship would be, so I could easily locate it on the return trip. Then I unloaded all my gear from the knapsack and placed it in the tent, with the exception of my money, gun, ammo and time machine. I wrote Sharon a note and left it in the tent. Then I took my knapsack and headed for civilization. About a mile down the trail, I spotted a hollowed out tree and I placed the time machine in it. I took a " GPS " reading and continued on my way.

It was a long cold walk and after hours of walking I finally arrived at Bratburg Road. You just can't imagine how good it felt to see cars going up and down the road.

Down the road I went, walking towards town. When I got to the little store, I stopped and went in and got a cup of coffee and a sandwich. I spent about thirty minutes there and then I walked on down the road. It wasn't long until I could see people walking up and down the sidewalks.

I walked on down the street to a little bike shop where I bought a moped. It didn't go very fast only about twenty five miles per hour, but it sure beat walking.

From there I went to a clothing store and bought me a heavy coat and some long johns. Then I went to Wal-mart and bought two heavy quilts. My last stop was a grocery store where I purchased lots of can food. With my knapsack fully loaded I headed back toward my tent.

I rode back up the hill until I reached the steep curve sign and I entered the forest. Riding through the forest was a lot of fun until I reached the swamp. As soon as I entered the swamp I went into a tail spin and got dumped in the mud. I painfully picked myself up and got back on the moped. The rest of the way across the swamp I held my speed down to five miles per hour. After exiting the swamp, I resumed my normal speed and about forty minutes later I arrived back at my tent.

The first thing that I did was look for signs of Sharon being here and there wasn't any. I sincerely hope she arrives soon so we can spend the rest of our wait period at a hotel in town. It wouldn't be very nice of me to go to a hotel without her and when she arrives, she's stuck out here by herself.

I stayed out there in my tent and waited for what seemed like forever. Days soon turned into weeks and weeks soon turned into months and Sharon still hasn't arrived. I have went over in my mind, a thousand times, did I set both time machines to the same setting. If I did so, where is Sharon?

It's now one week away from the spaceships arrival time and it looks like I will have to do this job on my own. This last week has been a very difficult one. I moved my tent back an extra hundred yards to make sure that I did not get hit with any debris from the crash. I hated the idea of doing this without Sharon; however I figured that once I hid the spaceship, time would change and I would see Sharon again.

This week slowly passed by and late one night, while I was sleeping in my tent, I heard a loud crashing sound and I knew the spaceship had arrived. Bright and early the next morning I got my camouflage blanket and walked over to the spaceship. I covered most of the ship including the blinking light, so our group wouldn't find it.

Within a matter of seconds, I was a young man again and part of our original camping party. I remembered everything that happened and I walked into my tent to see if Sharon remembered. What I saw next about sent me into shock. Sharon wasn't my date any more, some other girl was and I had no idea who she is.

CHAPTER ELEVEN

SOMETHING AIN"T RIGHT

CHAPTER ELEVEN

I gave her a big smile and quickly backed out of the tent. Standing across from me was two of my lovers, Alice and Betty and neither one of them remembered a thing about what happened. Also standing around me was all my previously dead friends. This was really weird and I did not have a clue on how to act. However, I had this unbelievable urge to give each and every one of then a big hug, but I thought better of it because they would think that I completely lost my mind.

It wasn't long until my new girl friend came out of the tent and I heard George call her Maria. At least now I know what to call her. Listening to the conversation, I figured out that this was to be our last night here and we were going home in the morning. Jerame kept saying that he wished this camping trip would go on forever. Mark had cooked us a very nice dinner and all of us sat down, relaxed and ate dinner. It wasn't too long afterwards, that the sun began to set and darkness had come upon us.

I knew that I had to go into our tent and spend the night with Maria and believe it or not it was kind of frightening. Maria was a very beautiful young girl and I had to go into the tent and pretend that she's my girl friend and make love to her.

I entered the tent and Maria was just lying there so I lay down on the blanket and we immediately started French kissing. After a minute or two I spoke up and said; Maria I love you and she got as mad as she could possibly get at me. She yelled; don't you call me Maria, only that dam George calls me Maria. My name is Marta, not Maria.

I quickly apologized and told her that I was sorry and I would never do it again. Within a moment or two, we went back to French kissing and making out in our tent. In all due respect, I must say that I had a wonderful time that night and I would never forget it. The next morning, I got up and left the tent and I felt like a new man. All of us came outside and had a hot cup of coffee, before we started loading up our gear.

Thirty minutes later, we had our gear fully loaded and we started our long walk back through the forest. As we walked along the trail and I listened to everyone talking, I realized one very important fact; everyone else believed that they had a wonderful week long camping trip. When in fact, this camping trip was anything but wonderful and as far as I was concerned, spanned over twelve years and had many, many weird nightmares in it.

The day went pretty fast and it wasn't long until we reached Bratburg Road. Four of us stayed there and watched all the gear, while the other four went to retrieve the cars.

An hour and a half later the cars arrived, we loaded our gear and we were on our way home. I would get to see my family again after being going twelve years and they would only think that I was away for one week. I let Marta drive my car because I had no idea where she lived and I could just sit back and let her drive herself home.

A short while later, we arrived at Marta's house and she unloaded her gear, told me that she had a great time and kissed me good bye. It was now time for me to return home to my family and I was scared that I would over react and break down crying when I got there. I have to act normal when I get inside so I pulled into the driveway and just sit there for a couple of minutes to get my composure. I exited the car and calmly walked inside the house.

As soon as I got inside the door and saw my mother and father standing there, I just lost it; I broke down crying and threw my arms around both of them. I knew that I would never be able to explain my behavior but I just couldn't help myself.

After a few minutes of crying, they both started asking what's wrong and I did not have any answer to give them. I just put a smile on my face and said; I just missed you two a lot.

Later, when my little brother and sister came home from school, I broke down again. I think my entire family suspects something happened to me on our camping trip and they are so very right, but there's absolutely no way in this world I could tell them about it and even if I did, they would just think that I am going nuts, and lost my mind.

I can't help but wonder what happened to Sharon. She somehow changed her own history and for that to happen, she must have gone a lot farther back in time than I went. I drove by her house and knocked on her door and some other family was living there. My life just isn't the same without Sharon being here.

I returned back to my house and at that very moment, I knew what I had to do. I had to wait another thirty days for all the creatures in the spaceship to die and retrieve the same time machine that she used and go back in time and rescue her. Over the next thirty days, I worked all kinds of jobs to get enough money to purchase a genuine space suit, from the space research labs.

I purchased a small solar panel to be used when recharging car batteries. Nearing the end of the thirty day waiting period, I had finally acquired the thirty two hundred dollars needed to purchase the space suit.

So one quiet day when no one was around, I gathered up my gear and headed back to the forest. This time around, I had no trouble finding the spaceship. The only thing I needed to do now was go inside and retrieve the appropriate time machine. I came prepared this time; I brought two hydraulic jacks to be used for turning the spaceship over. Slowly but surely, I managed to turn over the spaceship.

As I pulled the door open, I heard a screeching sound and one of those creatures flew out. It immediately went straight for my neck and I quickly slapped it away. Then it took off flying through the forest. Darn creature scared me half to death, so into the spaceship I ran and pulled the door shut. Thank goodness that there was only one creature in here.

How could that creature still be alive? The original creature must live a lot longer than those fifteen days. At that very moment, I realized that once again, I turned that creature loose on the world.

I now only have about one hour to get the time machine that Sharon used, and leave here. Moving as fast as I could I got all my gear on and hooked up. I set the gauge on the time machine for one year. I stepped out of the spaceship and pushed the button. About two seconds later, I was there. I took a " GPS ' reading and discovered that I have traveled twelve years. Upon Realizing that this time machine travels twelve times as far as the other one did, with the same exact setting. I took a few extra minutes to calculate my new time setting and get it punched in.

I pushed the button again, and away I went traveling through time. Approximately ten minutes later I came to a complete stop.

CHAPTER TWELVE

RESCUEING SHARON

CHAPTER TWELVE

I found myself going head over heels, for two or three flip flops through the bushes. Wow, what a rough landing, it's a miracle that I didn't break my neck.

I took a quick look around and I was pretty sure that I was here ahead of Sharon. There is a big maple tree standing right where the oak tree used to be. If you couldn't identify yours trees, you would never know it wasn't the same tree.

They say that every person has at least one great soul mate in their lives and Sharon is mine. I just could not imagine going through life without her and I sincerely hope she feels the same way about me. It doesn't matter how long I have to wait because as soon as she arrives, I will be here to rescue her. The first thing that I have to do is walk out and find out what year it is now. I hung a piece of cloth on the tree.

I set up my tent and left Sharon a detailed message sitting on the floor of the tent. The message stated that she traveled a lot further back in time than I did and that she somehow changed her own history and in the future she does not exist anymore.

The message also stated that I changed the events of the first invasion of those creatures, however I went back to the spaceship to get another time machine and when I opened the ship; one of those creatures was still alive and flew out. I think the invasion started all over again. Anyway, I am here now and I am going to walk into town and see what year it is. Hopefully, I will see you here when I get back.

After finishing my letter, I ventured on through the forest, making my way to the nearest town. The entire forest looked different, everything had completely changed. When I got to the spot where the swamp used to be, there was no swamp. It was just a bunch of high weeds.

I continued on towards Bratburg Road and a short while later I was standing right where Bratburg Road used to be. The road was gone and this presented a problem, if there is a town down there, I was going to have to traverse many miles of new forest, to get there. Also finding my way back to where the spaceship crashed, would be a problem.

I had a red magic marker with me so I began marking the trees. On the bark of the tree, that was standing right where the steep curve sign used to be, I placed about a dozen red marks all over the tree.

Continuing on my way through the forest, I would mark a tree every fifty feet or so, with an arrow pointed in the right direction. It wasn't an easy walk because I found myself having to go up and down a lot of hills and cross some very rough terrain. After many hours of walking and marking trees, I finally caught sight of a small western style town up ahead. I tucked in my shirt and walked straight into town.

The entire town was no more than one hundred buildings in size. There was one store, one bar and one horse stable. All the other buildings appeared to be houses.

I asked the first person that I met, while walking down the town road, what is today's date? I told that person that I had been camped out in the wilderness for a couple of years and lost track of time. The stranger replied; April seventh. Then I asked; what year? He replied; eighteen eighty three. I thanked him and continued on my way.

I have money on me, but the money I have is no good in this time period. Since I need supplies, the best thing for me to do is find a job.

Upon entering the general store, I ask the manager if he was hiring any help. He told me that I was in luck, his other helper had got himself killed four days ago and he was looking for a new helper. Naturally I asked, what happened to him?

The store owner replied; a gunfighter by the name of Jack Barton forced him into a gunfight and then killed him. I replied; don't you have any law around here? The store owner answered; we did have, Jack Barton killed him two months ago.

I replied; no difference, I will take the job anyway. The store owner then informed me, that it pays fifty cents per day and I immediately thought, wow, he's the last of the big time spenders.

The first thing I needed was a gun and the store owner sold them. Fortunately for me, I could buy a decent hand gun for one dollar and fifty cents. Three days after I went to work there, I was able to purchase a hand gun with a holster and I began wearing it around town. Two days later, Jack Barton rode back into town and he went to all three businesses and made them pay him protection money. I could not believe this, everybody in town was afraid of him. Jack Barton was a real piece of garbage.

He stayed in town for one night and two days and right before he left, he went into the bar, or should I say saloon as they called it in these days and he forced a man to draw his gun.

Jack told the man, that he was going to kill him anyway, so he might as well draw his gun and try his luck. The man panicked, drew his gun and Jack Barton killed him. Then jack laughed, told everyone in the saloon that he would see them in a couple of weeks. Then he got on his horse and rode out of town.

I have to be extremely careful here because Sharon's history got changed. Since I came to this time period and arrived here ahead of Sharon, it could very well be possible that it was me who changed her history. Who knows Jack Barton might be one of her relatives and if I kill him, I also kill her. The best thing for me to do, is just stay out of his way. Who knows, I might have another couple of months to wait, before Sharon arrives.

I hung around town and worked for another month and it was now time for me to venture back to my camp site and check to see if Sharon had arrived. I told my boss that I needed a few days off and I left town. Following my red markings back to my camp site, turned out to be pretty simple. They led me straight back to the tree, where the steep curve sign used to be. From there I entered the main forest and made my way back to the camp site. My tent was still standing and the only cloth hanging on the tree branch was mine. Now, I know for a fact that Sharon hasn't arrived yet.

I wrote Sharon another letter and told her what she needed to know about town and the people that I have met there. I told her about the crazy gunfighter named Jack Barton and what he is doing to this town. Last but not least, I told Sharon that I would venture up here at least once every month and check to see if she had arrived yet. I spent the night in the tent and the next morning I got up pretty early and started practicing my draw, just in case I get forced into a gunfight. Considering myself a marksman with a pistol, the only thing I lack is the speed of the draw.

I spent hours doing nothing but drawing and holstering my gun. After a while, I came to one conclusion, I am fast, real fast. Now it's time to practice drawing and firing my gun. I set up an empty can, drew my gun and fired; I missed it by three inches. That's not to bad being I was twenty five feet away.

Over and over again I practiced until I could hit the can every time. The truth be told, I have become pretty good with a gun. I spent one more night in camp, and then I gathered my gear and went back to town. Jack Barton, the gunfighter was still out of town so everything in town seemed to be nice and quiet.

By the time I got back into town, it was pretty late, so I went straight to the barn, where I have been sleeping. I got myself a good night's sleep. I like my boss at the store where I work because he's a pretty nice guy. Not only did he give me a job but he also lets me sleep in his barn. The next morning at nine o'clock, I went back to work. My job consists of loading people's wagons with their food and supplies.

My day was pretty uneventful until three o'clock when Jack Barton rode back into town. He went straight to the saloon and drank beer for the next couple hours. I got off duty at five o'clock and went back to the barn to relax. At seven o'clock Jack Barton grabbed one of the local town women, took her behind a house and raped her.

The next day, it's the talk of the town. Everyone knows Jack Barton done it, but nobody does anything about it. Unbelievable, this whole town is afraid of him.

Early the next morning, Jack Barton goes to the three local businesses and makes his collections. He made the stable owner pay him a dollar, he made the saloon owner pay him ten dollars and he made my boss, the store owner, pay him a dollar. It appears my boss didn't move fast enough for him, because Jack Barton cracked him upside his head with his gun butt. I am trying desperately hard to stay out of trouble but that gunfighter is really pissing me off.

If I screw up and shoot one of Sharon's relatives, Sharon would not exist anymore, even worse, if I shoot one of my relatives, no more me. It was at this point that I made up my mind, Jack Barton better stay away from me or he's going to get what he deserves. Consequences or not, if he screws with me he's going to die.

Later that day, Jack Barton got on his horse and rode back out of town. For the next couple of weeks, everything was peaceful again until one bright sunny day, when Jack Barton came riding back into town.

I was in the store working, when Jack Barton came into the store to collect his protection money. He came walking over to the front of the store, looked at me and smiled and then he said; who the hell, do you think you are looking at? I quickly told him that I was looking at a yellow belly, dead beat piece of garbage. Then I informed him that he would not be entering this store, not now or ever.

He asked me; who's going to stop me? I replied; that would be me. We both walked to the middle of the street. I used to watch a lot of movies on television and my favorite shows were westerns, so I knew exactly what I had to do.

I told him; my name is Mike Ortman and my friends call me " the widow maker " and I think you ought to know the name of the man that's going to kill you. All of a sudden, I could see a worried look on his face. It appears that he's not used to having someone stand up to him.

I began slowly circling him to his right and I told him to make his move. Once again I laughed and called him a coward. By this time, everyone in town was outside to watch the gunfight. Jack Barton knew that he couldn't back down now and he reached for his gun. Within a heartbeat, I reached for mine. Jack Barton thought he was fast, but he never even cleared his leather holster before I popped a shot into his chest and he began staggering backwards.

All of a sudden, I hear another shot go off and I watched Jack Barton hit the ground. I turned and standing behind me but off to one side, was Sharon. She had arrived earlier and walked into town. Sharon saw me, in the middle of the street, facing down a gunfighter and she thought I was in trouble and she quickly pulled her gun and popped a slug into Jack Barton's chest.

   Within seconds, the whole town was cheering. I watched Sharon for a couple of minutes, just to make sure she didn't vanish. When I was sure, that I hadn't killed one of her relatives and Sharon was okay, I ran straight to her and gave her the biggest hug that I could ever give her, along with many, many kisses.

   The women of the town were offering us free meals, the saloon was offering us all the free drinks that we could drink, and instantly, I found myself being the town hero. I introduced Sharon, to the whole town as my wife and soon the partying began.

We went over to one woman's house and had this fantastic dinner. Then we went over to the saloon and started the main party. Sharon and I have never drunk any alcoholic beverages before and this was to be our first time. As soon as we got inside, the free drinks started coming. All the people inside the saloon were buying us free drinks and the saloon owner himself, was sending us free drinks. It wasn't very long at all until Sharon and I were both smashed. We said good night to everyone in the saloon, and then we went to the barn and crashed.

The next morning, we woke up and both of us had these terrible headaches. We crawled out of the hay and made our way outside. Sharon and I could definitely use some aspirins, but the only store in town doesn't carry any. I guess Sharon and I will just have to start walking and hope these headaches go away. I stopped by my boss's house and informed him that I was leaving town. He invited us in for a cup of coffee and thanked me for a job well done.

We were walking through town waving at everyone and saying goodbye to all the towns people when someone yelled out; widow maker. I froze in my tracks and told Sharon to move off the street. After raising my hands in the air, I slowly turned. Then I lowered my hands back to my side.

There was a stranger standing there and he asked me; was I that famous gunfighter known as the widow maker? I replied; that would be me. The stranger then said; you cost me two hundred dollars. I replied; how did I cost you two hundred dollars? The stranger then replied; the good people of this town, offered me two hundred dollars to come here and kill Jack Barton, but when I got here, I found out you already killed him.

By this time, the town's people had gathered all around to watch the upcoming gunfight. Then the stranger said; maybe I will just take the two hundred dollars from you. I answered; you can try, but that will cost you a lot more than two hundred dollars.

I started to circle to his right and he smiled and said; relax, I am not here for a gunfight; I just wanted to meet the famous gunfighter known as the widow maker.

  The stranger then said; what kind of gunfighter walks everywhere and doesn't ride a horse? Just out of curiosity, why don't you ride a horse? I looked at him with a big smile on my face and said; too dangerous.

  Everybody in town started laughing and then the stranger started laughing. He laughed so hard that he started choking and couldn't catch his breath. After three or four minutes, he stopped choking and looked at me and said; you are something else. Then he turned and walked away.

  I watched him walk into the saloon and then I asked one of the town's people standing there, who is he? The guy laughed and said; That's Doctor John Holliday, he's one of the fastest guns alive.

Sharon and I continued on our way out of town and as soon as we were out of sight, Sharon began yelling at me; are you crazy? Do you want to get yourself killed? Then she said; having a gunfight with Doc Holiday, is the surest way I know to get killed.

I laughed at all of Sharon's remarks and we continued on our way. We followed all the red arrows and eventually we made it back to the main tree that was marked with dozens of red marks. We took a short break there and then we made our way back to our camping spot.

Sharon told me that her time machine had vanished just after she arrived here. That means the two of us have to travel back to our time with only one time machine. Doing that could be very dangerous, but I don't see where we have any choice in the matter.

I took the solar panel out of the tent and put it together. Then I placed it into the direct sunlight and hooked our battery to it. In about twelve hours the battery should be fully charged.

   Meanwhile, I started explaining some things to Sharon about this journey.   I said; Sharon, you know it's true, you do become just like the people in your environment. I came to this period of time with plans to completely stay out of trouble. Because I was stuck here for two months, everything changed and I become like everyone else. Only in my case, I became a gunfighter.

CHAPTER THIRTEEN

BACK TO OUR FUTURE

CHAPTER THIRTEEN

Sharon and I spent the night here and relaxed. Bright and early the next morning, we put our space suits on and gathered our gear for the trip home.

I hooked up the battery to the time machine and asked Sharon if she was ready. Sharon put her arms around me and I put my arms around her. I told Sharon to hold on tight and I pushed the button.

We went zooming through time. Only this time we were kind of off balance and we started spinning in circles. Sharon and I were going around and around and we were getting dizzier by the minute. I said to Sharon; hold me tight and don't let go.

About that time I started vomiting and so did Sharon. The vomit would shoot straight out and vanish as it stopped in that time period.

Finally we came to a screeching stop and the two of us went rolling through the bushes. Sharon and I just laid there and moaned and groaned. We were so dizzy that neither one of us could stand up for at least ten minutes.

The spaceship was already there and covered with a camouflage blanket. About three seconds later we zoomed out of that spot and instantly we found ourselves back on the original camping trip.

I found myself standing there looking at all my friends again and I remembered everything that happened. I did not see Sharon so she must be in the tent. After crossing my fingers, I opened the tent and went in.

This time, we got it right, Sharon was inside and she was young again. Just like me, Sharon had remembered everything we went through on our time travel journeys. The next day, we ended our camping trip and went home. This time it was Sharon, who was crying like a baby, when she saw her family.

Later that day, Sharon's mother called my house and wanted to know, if anything happened to Sharon on our camping trip.   That question caught me off guard, so I told her that Sharon got extremely home sick from being away so long.

   Two days later Sharon calls me and tells me to turn on the news station.   I flipped the channel and my heart just about dropped to my feet.   There was a presidential speech taking place.   The only problem, it wasn't President James William Tate doing the talking.   It was President Donald Trump and when we left here our country was at peace and now our soldiers are fighting in Iraq and Afghanistan.   Our main problem being that there isn't anything that we could do to change it back.

   Sharon and I still have to stop the end of the world from happening again in less than thirty days.   The earlier version of me accidentally released one of those creatures back out into the world.   I called Sharon to try and get some good ideas on how to stop the end of the world from happening again.

Sharon and I discussed the problem and we were unable to come up with a plan. Since the time machine was in the space ship and the younger version of me went inside and tried to get it out and later took off to save Sharon, after accidently releasing the creature. This presented a big problem. How do we kill the creature that's inside the spaceship now?

Later that day, Sharon came over for a visit and the two of us went out together. We went to the hardware store and we were looking for anything that we could use to kill the creature. That's when I saw it, roach bombs, and I said to Sharon; there's our answer right there. Sharon looked back at me and said; yes I think you are right, that should do the trick. We purchased two of them and took them back to my house.

Later Sharon and I were discussing getting some explosives, so we could blow up the spaceship and prevent its future discovery. That's when Sharon started telling me about a man that lives in her neighborhood which claims that he can get anything you want.

The next day I hung around in Sharon's neighborhood watching for this guy. At eleven o'clock in the morning, I spotted him coming out of his house. I approached him and asked; I hear tell that you're the man that can get anything that I need, is that true? He checked me out for a minute, then he replied; maybe, what do you need?

I told the man that I needed five sticks of dynamite wrapped together with a five minute timer. He says; wow, no one's ever asked me for that before, I guess you are going to blow someone up, right? I didn't answer him so he replied; I can get that for you, but it will cost you five hundred bucks. He then tells me to meet him back here in a week, next Wednesday at twelve noon and bring the money.

I left and contacted Sharon and told her we needed five hundred dollars and we only have a week to get it. Sharon replied; I will get my half of the money.

We both went looking for work and I ended up waiting at a meeting spot in town. It was a spot where employers come and find day laborers.

I got lucky on my first day there; an employer picked me up and took me to his job. At the end of the day, he told me that he liked my work and he would pick me up there every day. He then handed a fifty dollar bill and said; good work. I met him there every day that week and I got my two hundred and fifty dollars.

Sharon wasn't as lucky as me and she could only get one hundred seventy five dollars. I told Sharon to barrow thirty five dollars from her parents and I would barrow forty dollars from mine. Eventually we came up with all the money we needed and I went back into Sharon's neighborhood and met the man on Wednesday. I gave him the five hundred dollars and he gave me the explosives. He told me to be careful, you push that button and five minutes later it blows up.

I put the explosives in my car and drove back to my house and waited down the block. After about a forty minute wait, I saw all my other family members come out and get into my father's car and drive off.

I took the explosives into my house and got a towel out of the closet. Wrapping the dynamite firmly in a towel, I then placed the towel into a plastic trash bag. I took the trash bag out in the yard, I got a shovel out of the shed and I buried the dynamite in the far right hand corner of my yard.

In case of an accidental explosion, I did not want anyone to get hurt, and in the rare event it did somehow go off out there, it would only blow up a section of our fence.

Sharon and I had planned hard and heavy this time and we hoped that this time we would get it right. This could be our last chance and we can't afford any more screw ups. We still have two and a half weeks to go before we can correct our big mistake and save the world.

Sharon and I started spending every single day together, trying to get a little enjoyment out of life while we still had a chance. We would go everywhere together, in fact, anywhere you seen one of us, you would also see the other. Each evening Sharon and I would go to my house for a little love making. Afterwards, we would discuss old times and how much we miss it. I would always find myself thinking about my other two wives, Alice and Betty and how much I miss them and our children.

Alice and Betty are truly the lucky ones because they don't have any memories of our relationships or our children. Every once in a while, when I see one of them on the street, I just want to go up to them and kiss them. I want to tell them that I love them very much. Unfortunately for me I can't, they would just think that I had lost my mind or that I was some kind of lovesick fool, even if we are the best of friends. Sharon told me that she also misses them a lot. Alice and Betty were part of our family for eleven years and Sharon says; it is like losing two deeply loved sisters.

Day after day I find myself more and more stressed out worrying about the bomb I buried in the back yard, hoping that none of my family members find it and blow themselves up.

I took Sharon out on the town, so we could sit back, enjoy ourselves and just relax. Later that day, while I had Sharon alone in my bedroom, I got down on my knees and ask Sharon to marry me. I said to Sharon; sweetheart, I don't have any money to buy you a ring because I spent it all buying the things we needed to save the entire population of the world. I love you very much and if you will have me and we survive the big event, I would love to marry you and make you my wife.

Sharon looked at me with a big smile on her face and said; yes I will marry you. Then she kissed me and said; I love you too. Sharon and I made love right after that.

Later that night, George Bateman called me at around two o'clock in the morning. He was crying and he said; Mary Zigler had a heart attack about an hour ago and they just pronounced her dead at the hospital. I told George that I was sorry to hear that and to let me know, when and where to go, on the funeral arrangements.

As soon as I hung up the phone, I started crying, I just couldn't help myself. Then I told Sharon what happened and she started crying.

Three days later they had the funeral and they ask me to be a pall bearer. Sharon and I were both at the funeral and paid our respects to her family and friends. Deep inside, Sharon and I had a guilty conscience, we knew that something would happen to her and we didn't warn her. Mary was the only member of our group that died of natural causes, when we were trying to run and hide from those creatures. However, looking back on the situation, she would not have believed us, if we tried to warn her.

All of my other friends were at the funeral too. They were paying their respects and crying. I took the liberty to give both Betty and Alice a big hug and a kiss without drawing to much attention to myself.

After the funeral, Sharon and I went back to my house and reflected on all the cute and funny things Mary had done in her short life.

The next night, Sharon and I met all our friends at a night club, where we drank beer and discussed Mary's life and told each other how much we would miss her. We were only there about an hour, when three strangers came in and tried hitting on all the girls while they were sitting with us. We warned the three men and told them to take a hike, but they wouldn't listen. Then one of them put his hand on Sharon and all hell broke loose. There were seven of us fighting inside the night club, the four of us guys and the three of them. The night club owner called the cops and all seven of us got arrested.

Needless to say, the three girls went home by themselves that night. The next morning they took the four of us in front of a judge for a bond hearing. The judge set a one hundred dollar bond on each of us. Later that evening the girls showed up and bonded us out.

I went home and caught hell from my parents after I tried to explain to them, what happened. My parents were right; we should not have been in the night club to start with.

Sharon and I have to be back at the spaceship in two days to prepare for the big event. Sometimes I find myself wondering if this world is really worth saving. My father told me, that he was tired of me always getting into trouble and ordered me to go out and find a job. Unfortunately for me, I cannot get a job until the big event has past and we are successful at avoiding the end of all mankind.

Bright and early the next morning, Sharon arrives back at my house with a big smile on her face and says; I am pregnant again. That was good news to me, so I grabbed Sharon and I hugged her and kissed her. Then I asked Sharon; are we going to name our little boy John this time? She smiled and said; absolutely.

We spent the next day hanging out together and enjoying life to its fullest, knowing that tomorrow is the day of the big event and it may bring forth even more problems.

The next day, Sharon and I met at a coffee shop, we each had a cup of coffee and then we rode up to the little store on Bratburg Road and left our car there. We took our gear and started walking up the road to the steep curve sign. A short time later we arrived at the sign and we entered the forest. Sharon and I walked until we were completely out of site from the main road. Then we took a snack break and a short rest.

CHAPTER FOURTEEN

THE FINAL CORRECTION

CHAPTER FOURTEEN

Sharon and I got to our feet and proceeded onward toward the spaceship. We made our way through the swamp, crossed the small river and walked through the forest until we arrived at the spaceship.

We set our camp up approximately a quarter mile away on the other side of the spaceship. The reason for doing this was to make sure the other me would not see us or know we were there.

We relaxed until just before night fall, then we took a roach bomb canister and stuck the tip of the spraying mechanism through a tiny hole in the ship and we set it off. The next day was similar to this one, we relaxed all day, and then at night fall, we set off the second canister of roach poison. Our plan was to kill the creature inside the spaceship before the other version of me shows up and opens the door.

The very next day, the other me showed up and he starts jacking up the spaceship to get the door way turned up and open. Sharon and I watched him from a distance as he gets the doorway open and goes inside. This time no creatures flew out of the ship and all was quiet until he come running back out and coughing real hard.

I just figured that there must be some residue from the roach bombs still in the ship. After watching him going in and out three or four more times, he finally emerged with the time machine. We watched as he hooked it up to his battery and goes zooming off through time. Sharon and I walked over to the spaceship; our plan is to take the other time machine and blow up the spacecraft.

Sharon and I enter the spaceship and I begin unbolting the time machine. We begin hearing strange noises and we can't figure out where they are coming from. The noise sounds like something pecking on the outside of the spaceship.

After a few minutes work, I managed to get the time machine unbolted and I handed it out to Sharon. She takes it a far distance from the ship and lays it down. Sharon gets the bomb and brings it to the ship and hands it to me. I took the bomb and placed it in the center of the ship. I then told Sharon; that the second I push this button, we run like hell; we only have five minutes to get far away.

Immediately after I told that to Sharon, we heard that strange noise again. We turned around to look and we see something trying to squeeze through a tiny hole in the spaceships frame. The hole wasn't any larger than a dime but somehow this thing squeezed through.

It was one of those creatures and it immediately started buzzing and came straight at me. Before I could even flinch, this creature stung me and attached its self to the side of my neck. I dropped to the floor of the ship in terrible pain.

I managed to slide over to where the bomb was located and I told Sharon to run. Sharon was already crying, she looked at me and said; I will always love you Mike and out the door she ran. I pushed the button and I lay directly over top the bomb. In a moment or two, I lost consciousness and slipped into a coma. Five minutes later the bomb exploded and blew the spaceship into tiny pieces. Mike's body had been totally disintegrated along with all the creatures inside of it.

Sharon hung around for hours and cried her heart out. Realizing that she had successfully saved all human life on this planet, she picked up the time machine and walked out of the forest.

Once Mike's family reported him missing, the police began questioning Sharon about his disappearance. Sharon could not tell Mikes family or the police what really happened, so she just pretended as if she had no idea what happened to Mike.

Mike's family called Sharon all the time and begged her to tell them where mike was. Sharon did the only thing she could do and kept her mouth shut. Nine months later, Sharon gave birth to a baby girl and she named her Connie Ortman. Conceived around the same day as her son was and even born on the same exact day. That goes to show you that nothing in this world is set in stone.

When it became imminent that the police were going to arrest Sharon and charge her with Mike's murder, Sharon disappeared. She left her baby with her mom and dad and vanished.

The police are saying that she can't hide forever and they will eventually catch her, have a trial and convict her for Mike Ortman's murder. But this just isn't true because I know she used her time machine and vanished through time.   **THE END**

PLEASE READ THE FOLLOWING EPILOG PAGES.

EPILOG

Hello, my name is James Gordon Masterson and I am the author of this novel. I acquired most of my information for this novel from Mike Ortman and his diaries. However, he died before the ending of this story so I acquired the ending of the story from Sharon Cordman's recollections.

For all you history buffs out there, in 1883, a gunfighter named Jack Barton was shot and killed while in a gun fight with a man who called himself " the widow maker ". Mike Ortman stated in his diary that the biggest mistake that he made throughout this whole ordeal was getting into that gunfight with Jack Barton and changing history. This mistake caused a change in Presidents to take place and played a major role in the wars that followed. Mike and Sharon gave up everything, their families, their lives and their freedom to save the world and should be recognized as heroes.

EPILOG

I was with Sharon when she found out that the police were on their way to her house to arrest her and she panicked. Watching her scampering to get suited up and hook up the battery to her time machine before the police could arrive, I felt so envious of her. Then when the final moment came and she pushed the button and I watched her vanish right before my eyes, I knew she would never get caught by the police.

I have heard quite a few rumors lately about a mysterious woman, who appears out of nowhere and rescues people in need. I find myself wondering could this be Sharon using her time machine to save the lives of many different people throughout history.

I sincerely hope you have enjoyed reading my book and I wish you all the best luck in the world.
Until we meet again;

James Gordon Masterson

Printed in Great Britain
by Amazon